T0165823

Murder Most
Divine

Murder Most Most

Divine

Ecclesiastical Tales of Unholy Crimes

Edited by

RALPH McINERNY and MARTIN H. GREENBERG

CUMBERLAND HOUSE
NASHVILLE, TENNESSEE

Published by Cumberland House Publishing, Inc., 431 Harding Industrial Drive, Nashville, TN 37211

Cover design: Gore Studio, Inc.
Text design: Mary Sanford

Library of Congress Cataloging-in-Publication Data
Murder most divine : ecclesiastical tales of unholy crimes / edited by Ralph McInerny and Martin H. Greenberg.
    p. cm.
  ISBN 1-58182-121-2 (alk. paper)
   1. Detective and mystery stories, American. 2. Clergy--Fiction. I. McInerny, Ralph M.
  PS374.D4 M857 2000
  813'.0872083522--dc21

                           00-064421

1 2 3 4 5 6 7—05 04 03 02 01 00